# This book belongs to:

. . . . . . . . . . . . . . . . . . . . . . . . . . . . . . . . . .

. . . . . . . . . . . . . . . . . . . . . . . . . . . . . . . . . .

Retold by Sue Graves
Illustrated by Priscilla Lamont

Reading consultants: Betty Root and Monica Hughes

This edition published by Parragon in 2010

Parragon
Queen Street House
4 Queen Street
Bath BA1 1HE, UK

ISBN 978-1-4454-1211-5

Printed in China

# Goldilocks
## and the
# Three Bears

Bath New York Singapore Hong Kong Cologne Delhi Melbourne

## Helping your child to read

These books are closely linked to recognized learning strategies. Their vocabulary has been carefully selected from the word lists recommended by educational experts.

### *Read the story*
Read the story
to your child
a few times.

> That morning, a little girl was walking
> in the woods.
> Her name was Goldilocks.
> She saw the three bears' cottage.
> "What a pretty cottage!" she said.
> "I'll look inside."
> Goldilocks went in.
>
> 12

### *Follow your finger*
Run your finger under
the text as you read.
Your child will soon begin to
follow the words with you.

## Look at the pictures
Talk about the pictures. They will
help your child to understand the story.

Goldilocks went in.

13

## Give it a try
Let your child
try reading the
large type on each
right-hand page.
It repeats a line
from the story.

## Join in
When your child is ready, encourage
him or her to join in with the main
story text. Shared reading is the first
step to reading alone.

Once there were three bears.
There was Daddy Bear, Mommy Bear,
and Baby Bear.
They lived in a cottage in the woods.

Once there were three bears.

One morning, Mommy Bear made
some hot porridge.
"Let's go for a walk while it cools," said
Daddy Bear.
So the three bears went out.

The three bears went out.

That morning, a little girl was walking
in the woods.
Her name was Goldilocks.
She saw the three bears' cottage.
"What a pretty cottage!" she said.
"I'll look inside."
Goldilocks went in.

Goldilocks went in.

Goldilocks saw three bowls of porridge.
She was hungry, so she tried some.
But Daddy Bear's porridge was
too hot.
Mommy Bear's porridge was too cold.
Then she tried Baby Bear's porridge.
The porridge was just right.
Goldilocks ate it all up!

The porridge was just right.

15

Then Goldilocks saw three chairs.
She was tired, so she sat down.
But Daddy Bear's chair was too hard.
Mommy Bear's chair was too soft.
Then she tried Baby Bear's chair.
The chair was just right.
But Goldilocks broke it!

The chair was just right.

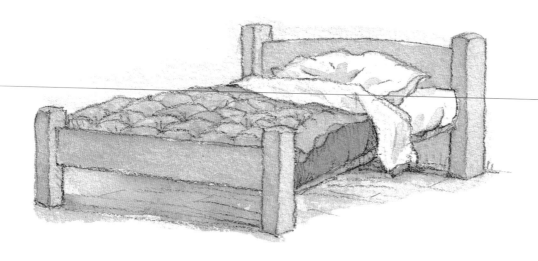

Goldilocks went upstairs.
She saw three beds.
She was sleepy, so she lay down.
But Daddy Bear's bed was too wide.
Mommy Bear's bed was too long.
Then she tried Baby Bear's bed.
The bed was just right.
Goldilocks fell asleep!

The bed was just right.

Then the three bears came back.
They looked at their porridge.
"Who's been eating my porridge?"
said Daddy Bear.
"Who's been eating my porridge?"
said Mommy Bear.
"Who's been eating my porridge,"
said Baby Bear, "and eaten it up?"

"Who's been eating my porridge?"

The three bears looked at their chairs.
"Who's been sitting in my chair?"
said Daddy Bear.
"Who's been sitting in my chair?"
said Mommy Bear.
"Who's been sitting in my chair,"
said Baby Bear, "and broken it?"

"Who's been sitting in my chair?"

The three bears went upstairs.
They looked at their beds.
"Who's been sleeping in my bed?"
said Daddy Bear.
"Who's been sleeping in my bed?"
said Mommy Bear.
"Who is sleeping in my bed?"
said Baby Bear. "She's still there!"

"Who is sleeping in my bed?"

Suddenly, Goldilocks woke up.
She saw the three bears.
They looked very angry.
Goldilocks ran away.
And the three bears never saw
her again!

Goldilocks ran away.

# Look back in your book.
## Can you read these words?

Mommy Bear

Daddy Bear

porridge

Baby Bear

Goldilocks

# Can you answer these questions?

What did Mommy
Bear make?

What happened
to Baby Bear's
chair?

Where did
the bears find
Goldilocks?

29

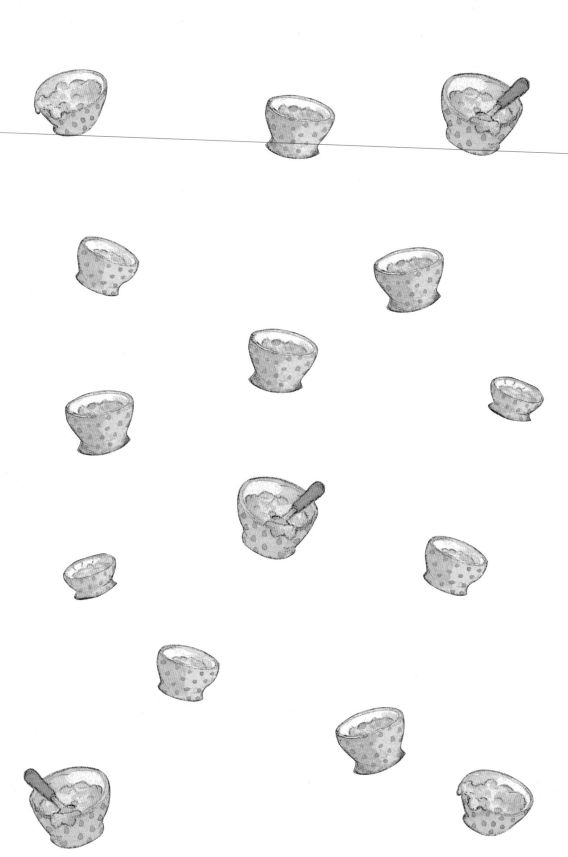